For Betty, Joyce, and Lisa—
mentors who cheered me on
—R.S.

For the filk music community, especially Allison
and Jodi, for helping me find my place onstage
—D.R.O.

Ruby Rose, Big Bravos

For information address HarperCollins Children's Books, a division of HarperCollins Publishers, 195 Broadway, New York, NY 10007.
www.harpercollinschildrens.com

ISBN 978-0-06-223571-8

The artist used Adobe Photoshop to create the illustrations for this book.
Typography by Jeanne L. Hogle
17 18 19 20 21 SCP 10 9 8 7 6 5 4 3 2 1
❖
First Edition

Ruby Rose

Big Bravos

By Rob Sanders · Illustrated by Debbie Ridpath Ohi

HARPER

An Imprint of HarperCollins*Publishers*

Today I woke up with the best idea ever.

"We're having a dance recital!" I told my dad.

"We are?" Dad answered.

I just knew he'd love the idea.

I tangled with my tights,

tugged on my tutu,

and tossed on my tiara.

"What's first?" I asked Bearishnikov.

He stared with his *you-know-what-to-do* look.

"You're right! We need posters!"

I pointed my toes and pliéd down the hall.

"Do we have paper and glitter?" I asked my dad.

He opened a drawer. "No messes, Ruby Rose," he said.

"No problem, Dad!"

I pirouetted back to my room, opened the window, and got busy.

Bearishnikov and I scribbled with markers, sketched roses, and sprinkled glitter.

As we finished, a breeze blew the curtains.

The posters fluttered . . . and flew . . . all around the room.

Bearishnikov stared.

I shrieked.

Dad showed up at the door.
"What a mess!" he said.

I got busy. This time cleaning my room.

When I was done, Bearishnikov and I decided to make tickets for the dance recital.

"But how will we deliver them?"

Bearishnikov looked at me.

"Brilliant!" I yelled.

We snipped paper tickets to invite everyone to the show.

We blew up balloons,

attached the tickets,

and let them soar.

"Ruby Rose!" Dad called.
"I'll clean it up," I called back.

I got busy again.

By the time I finished . . .

sprinkle, *sprinkle*, *sprinkle*.

Bearishnikov and I found our music, fitted our costumes, and fluffed up tissue-paper roses.

"Dad, can we make a stage?"

"Yes," he said, "but . . ."

"No messes!" I added.

I shoved the sofa,

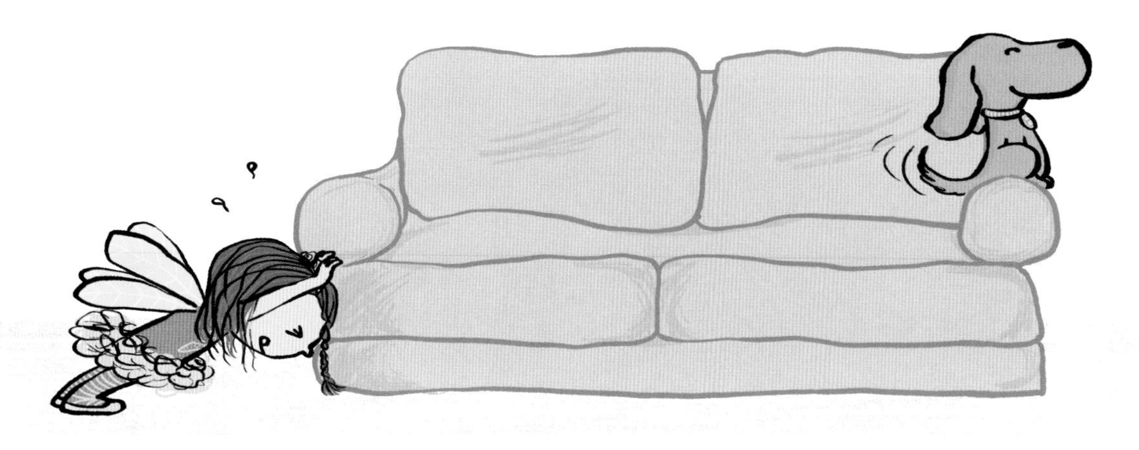

slid back the chairs,

and scooted the plants.

No problem. No mess.
It was almost recital time.

Bearishnikov and I hurried to get ready and stretched.

Dancers always need a good stretch.

"Ladies and gentlemen," I announced from my doorway, "introducing Ruby Rose and Bearishnikov!"

We promenaded into the living room and bowed.

Dad clapped.
I gulped.
"Where's Mom and the audience?"
"Caught in the rain," Dad answered.

I hugged Bearishnikov. "This is a problem."

Lightning flashed.
The lights flickered, then went off.

"This is a mess!" I groaned.

Bearishnikov and I slumped back to the bedroom.

The rain pounded. We pouted. Then there was a knock at the door.

"Ruby Rose," Dad began, "showtime."
I looked at Bearishnikov.

"You're right. We can't let down our fans—
even if we just have one."

Bearishnikov and I walked slowly from the bedroom and onto the stage.

There was more thunder.

CLAP, CLAP!

Or was that applause?
The rain didn't get in the way of my recital after all.

I twirled.

Bearishnikov swirled.

"Bravo!" cheered the crowd. *"Bravo!"*

We pranced and pranced.

"BRAVO!
BRAVO!"

We danced

and danced

and danced.

The audience clapped and chanted, *"Bravo! Bravo!"*

They showered us with ruby-red roses.

Everyone said it was the best dance recital ever.

Later that night, I tangled
with my tights,

tugged on my PJs,

and tossed off my tiara.

"Bearishnikov," I whispered. "That was the best idea ever!"

He snuggled close. I knew he thought so, too.